The Seven Chinese Brothers

The Seven Chinese Brothers

by MARGARET MAHY

Illustrated by Jean and Mou-sien Tseng

SCHOLASTIC INC.

New York Toronto London Auckland Sydney
Mexico City New Delhi Hong Kong Buenos Aires

This book was originally published in hardcover by Scholastic Press in 1990.

ISBN-13: 978-0-590-42057-0
ISBN-10: 0-590-42057-7

54 53 52 51 50 49   17 18 19 20/0

Printed in the U.S.A.   40

Title page calligraphy by Jeanyee Wong

Design by Claire Counihan

Editor's Note About *The Seven Chinese Brothers*

Although the seven brothers are fictive characters in the classic tall-tale tradition, Emperor Ch'in Shih Huang (Qin Shi Huang) 259–210 B.C. figures prominently as chief antagonist in this Han tale. Ch'in Shih Huang is generally credited with having brought about the unification of China by establishing rule over rival states under one central government.

It was also Ch'in Shih Huang who planned the construction of the Great Wall, a monumental undertaking that began during his reign and continued in subsequent centuries of dynastic rule. Stretching nearly 4,000 miles (6,400 kilometers) across northern China, the Great Wall was meant to be a defense against border invaders from the north. Handmade of stone, brick, and earth, the Great Wall is the longest structure ever built. Building the Great Wall was an arduous, backbreaking, often extremely dangerous task that exacted a death toll on thousands upon thousands of conscripted laborers. It is the very suffering of the workers that sparks our seven heroes to use their special powers to intervene on the people's behalf.

In this story, justice is served, and the tyrannical Emperor Ch'in Shih Huang meets an untimely end at the hands (tears, rather) of the Seventh Brother. In actuality, history reports that Ch'in Shih Huang probably died in 210 B.C. while on an inspection tour of the empire, just eleven years after consolidating power. However cruel, Emperor Ch'in Shih Huang remains one of the most colorful personages in Chinese history.

The incense burner has been lit. We invite you to step hundreds of centuries back in time, into the splendor and pageantry of the first imperial court of all China, to meet the notorious Ch'in Shih Huang and seven extraordinarily gifted brothers.

Once upon a time, when Ch'in Shih Huang was emperor
of all China, seven remarkable brothers lived together
on a beautiful hillside. They walked alike, they talked alike,
they even looked so much alike that it was hard to tell
one brother from the brother next to him. All the same,
each brother had something special about him. Each brother
had one amazing power that was all his own.

First Brother's amazing ears could hear a fly sneeze from a hundred miles away, while Second Brother's amazing eyes could look right across the hundred miles and see the fly sitting on the Great Wall of China, sneezing and feeling very sorry for itself. Third Brother was a man of unusual strength. He could walk across China in a straight line, lifting up any mountains that got in his way and putting them carefully back behind him. Fourth Brother was strong, too, for he had bones of iron that wouldn't break, buckle, or bend.

Fifth Brother had legs that could grow as tall and thick as tree trunks, while Sixth Brother never, ever became too hot, no matter how hard he worked under the summer sun. As for Seventh Brother, he was the baby of the family, and all his six older brothers tried to keep him smiling and happy. For he was their youngest brother, and when he was unhappy he wept great big warm salt tears, and each tear was large enough to drown an entire village.

The seven brothers lived very happily together, and Seventh Brother never once had anything to cry about. But one day as they worked on their hillside, First Brother lifted his head (with his amazing ears on either side of it) and said, "I can hear such a moaning and a groaning one hundred miles away, by the Great Wall of China. Second Brother, take a look and tell me what all the trouble is about."

Second Brother turned his far-seeing eyes toward the Great Wall. "Ai ya!" he cried. "There is an enormous hole in the Great Wall of China! I see a hundred poor men working, working day and night, night and day. They look so tired and weak. Perhaps they are not allowed to sleep or eat until the hole in the Great Wall of China is repaired."

"Ai ya! I can't bear it," cried Seventh Brother, who was always hungry himself. He looked as if he might begin to cry in sympathy with the poor, hardworking men.

"Don't cry!" said Third Brother quickly. "I'll go and help them." Off he went as quickly as he could, and got there in half a minute, less than no time.

He set to work at once, tossing great stones from one hand to the other as if they were feathers. By the time darkness came, the hole was completely filled. Then Third Brother lay down to take a nap.

But when the emperor heard that a single man had repaired the hole in one afternoon, he was not at all grateful. Indeed, he looked very worried.

"A man as powerful as that is more trouble than he's worth," thought the emperor to himself. "Strong men can be very useful to an emperor, but this one is *too* strong. One army may not be enough to catch him. I had better send two."

When Third Brother woke up from his nap, he found himself surrounded by two armies!

"By the command of the Celestial Emperor (whose face is more dazzling than the rising sun) you are to be executed in the morning," proclaimed the generals of the two armies. "Take the prisoner to the palace of the emperor!" they ordered.

When he heard this, Third Brother burst into tears.

A hundred miles away on the beautiful hillside,
First Brother heard Third Brother crying.

"Third Brother must be in trouble!" he exclaimed.
Second Brother looked far into the distance.

"Ai ya! Third Brother has been taken to the palace!
He's surrounded by two armies! They are going to execute
him in the morning. No wonder he is crying."

"Don't worry!" cried Fourth Brother, who saw
that Seventh Brother was about to cry, too. "I will change
places with him. The Celestial Emperor (whose face
is more dazzling than the rising sun) can try cutting
my head off as many times as he likes. Perhaps that will
make him feel better."

Off he went as quickly as he could, and got there
in half a minute, less than no time. He sneaked in between
the two armies to Third Brother, who was wide awake
and waiting for him.

So Third Brother went home, and Fourth Brother
took his place.

All the next day the officers of the two armies tried over and over again to behead Fourth Brother, but sword after sword bent and broke on his bones of iron. In the end, they were forced to confess to the mighty emperor (whose whisper was like the rumble of thunder) that they simply could not behead their prisoner.

"A man with bones of iron!" roared the mighty emperor. "Drown him in the deep sea! Tomorrow!"

When Fourth Brother heard that he was to be drowned, he became very upset.

"Bones of iron won't bend or buckle or break, but they will sink," he thought to himself, and he burst into tears.

A hundred miles away on the beautiful hillside, First Brother heard Fourth Brother begin to cry.

"Fourth Brother is crying," he said. Second Brother looked into the distance, far beyond the hills and said, "Ai ya! Tomorrow morning they are going to drown Fourth Brother. No wonder he is crying."

"Don't worry," Fifth Brother interrupted. "I will change places with him. The mighty emperor (whose whisper is like the rumble of thunder) can try to drown me as many times as he likes. Perhaps that might make him feel better."

Off he went, as quickly as he could, and got there in half a minute, less than no time. He tiptoed past the guards to Fourth Brother, who was awake and waiting for him. Swiftly, they switched places, and Fourth Brother went home.

All the next day the soldiers of the two armies tried to drown Fifth Brother. They threw him into the deep sea, but his legs grew so quickly, the water only came up to his knees.

They tried throwing him into deeper water, but the deep, deep water only just reached as far as his waist.

Finally, they threw him into the deepest part of the sea, but even the deepest part of the sea only came up to his neck. Waves broke under his chin.

"Ahhhh," said Fifth Brother, smiling happily. "How lovely and cool is the deepest seawater of all."

"He is more dangerous than I imagined," muttered the splendid emperor (whose merest glance was like a flash of lightning). "He won't drown, but he might burn. Into the fire with him, tomorrow morning!" he commanded.

When he was told his fate, Fifth Brother burst into tears.

Far away on the beautiful hillside, First Brother heard Fifth Brother's cries. Second Brother looked right across a hundred miles to the Great Wall of China.

"Ai ya!" he cried. "Tomorrow morning they are going to burn Fifth Brother alive. No wonder he is crying."

"Don't worry," said Sixth Brother, afraid that Seventh Brother might begin to cry, too. "I will take his place. The splendid emperor (whose merest glance is like a flash of lightning) can bake me all day long if he likes," he said with a shiver. "Perhaps that will make him feel better."

Off he went, as quickly as he could, and got there in half a minute, less than no time. He tiptoed in between the two armies and found Fifth Brother, who was awake and waiting for him.

So Fifth Brother went home, and Sixth Brother took his place.

The next day the two armies ran backwards and forwards, bringing kindling wood, brushwood and driftwood, and bundles of dried grass. They built such a big fire that the smoke from it drifted from one end of China to the other. But Sixth Brother never, ever felt too hot. Basking in the heat of the blaze, he sighed with happiness.

"How kind of the noble emperor to let me warm myself in his very own fire!" he cried.

The noble emperor (whose slightest frown
made the land shake like an earthquake) was furious.
"Send for the royal archers!" he ordered. "In the morning,
we will shoot this man full of arrows."

Sixth Brother burst into tears.

Over on the beautiful hillside, First Brother heard Sixth Brother crying. "Second Brother," he asked, "what do you see?"

"Ai ya!" cried Second Brother. "Tomorrow morning they are going to shoot Sixth Brother full of arrows."

The brothers looked at each other. "There is nothing for it," said First Brother. "We cannot leave Sixth Brother to die alone. We will all go to the noble emperor (whose slightest frown makes the land shake like an earthquake). He can shoot arrows through all of us. At least we will be together."

The brothers started their journey to the palace, but poor Seventh Brother was so upset, that he couldn't help crying just a little. His first tear was as big as the longest river in China, rolled into a single drop. His second tear was as big as the second longest river. Both tears were as salty as the sea.

A great ocean of warm saltwater swept down the road ahead of the brothers. It swept on for a hundred miles.

Seventh Brother's first tear swept one army north.
His second tear swept the other army south.

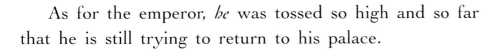

As for the emperor, *he* was tossed so high and so far
that he is still trying to return to his palace.

Seventh Brother's flood of tears swept over the Great Wall
of China, flowed all the way out into the Yellow Sea,
and all the way back again in half a minute, less than no time.

Sixth Brother was free!

He hurried back up the road while his six wonderful
brothers hurried down the road. They were
reunited at the Great Wall.

"Fish!" cried Fifth Brother. The wave had washed hundreds of glistening fishes ashore. There they were, flipping and flapping, piled all the way up to his knees.

"Wood!" cried Third Brother, gathering a forest to start a fire.

Fourth Brother snapped his iron finger and his iron thumb. A spark leaped out to set the fire blazing and crackling.

"Fire!" he cried, laughing.

"Oh, I'm so hungry," said Seventh Brother. "Now that we are all together again, we can have dinner and forget our troubles. I promise never to cry again, unless I absolutely must."

So the seven Chinese brothers sat themselves down
around the warm fire and feasted on delicious fried fish...
for after such a worrying week they were all very, very hungry.